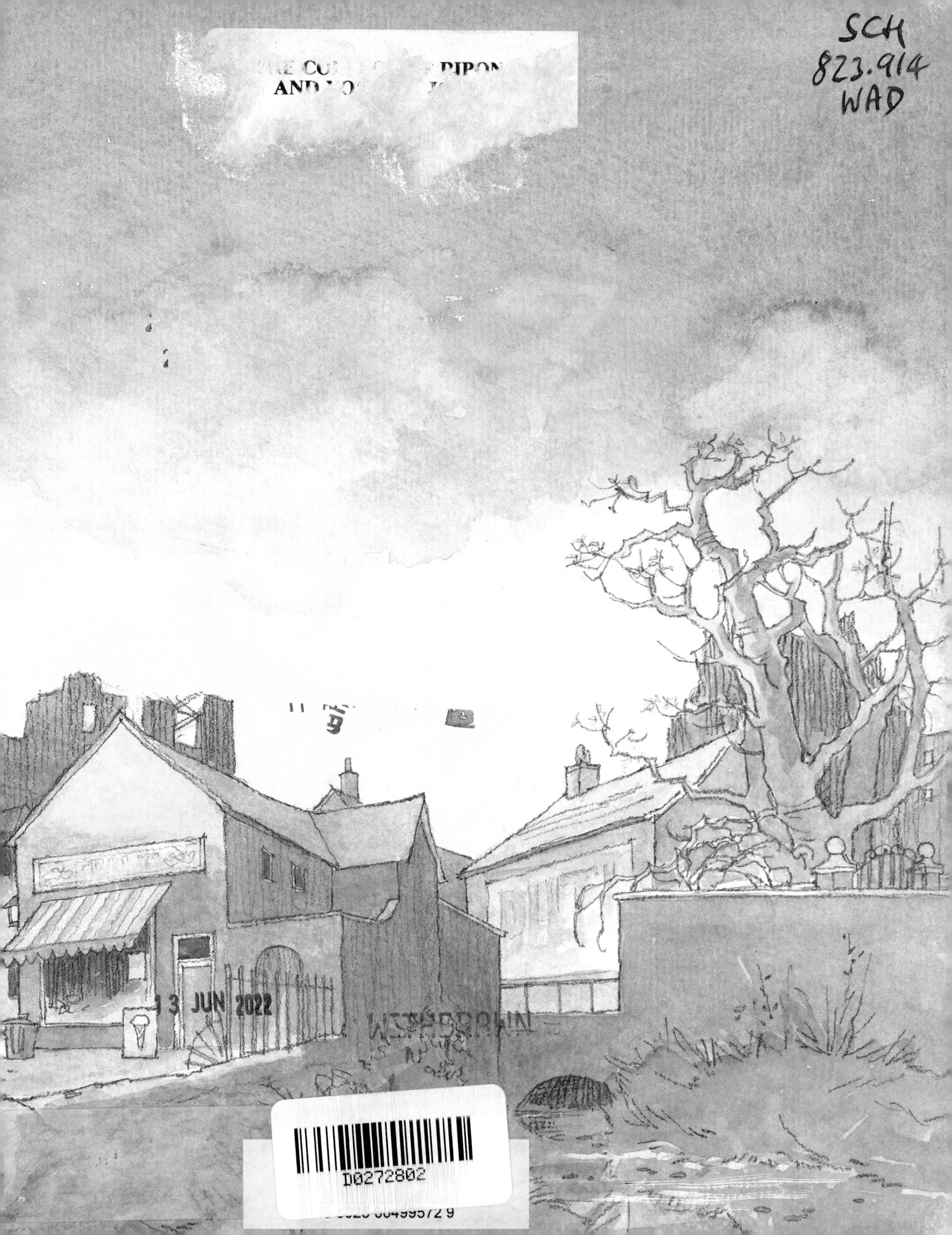

For Noreen
M.W.

First published 1989 by
Walker Books Ltd, 87 Vauxhall Walk
London SE11 5HJ

Text © 1989 Martin Waddell
Illustrations © 1989 Barbara Firth

First printed 1989   Reprinted 1989
Printed and bound by L.E.G.O., Vicenza, Italy

British Library Cataloguing in Publication Data
Waddell, Martin
The park in the dark
I. Title   II. Firth, Barbara
823'.914 [J]   PZ7

ISBN 0-7445-0716-2

The Park in the Dark

written by

Martin Waddell

illustrated by

Barbara Firth

WALKER BOOKS
LONDON

When the sun goes down
and the moon comes up
and the old swing creaks
in the dark,
that's when we go
to the park,
me and Loopy
  and Little Gee,
    all three.

Softly down the staircase,

through the haunty hall,

trying to look

small,

me and Loopy

and Little Gee,

we three.

It's shivery

out in the dark

on our way to the park,

down dustbin alley,

past the ruined mill,

so still,

just me and Loopy

and Little Gee,

just three.

And Little Gee
doesn't like it.
He's scared
of the things
he might see
in the park
in the dark
with Loopy and me.
That's me and Loopy
and Little Gee,
the three.

There might be

moon witches

or man-eating trees

or withers that wobble

or old Scrawny Shins

or hairy hobgoblins,

or black boggarts' knees

in the trees,

or things we can't see,

me and Loopy

and Little Gee,

all three.

But there's not,

says Loopy,

and I agree,

and Little Gee

gets up on my back and

we pass the Howl Tree,

me and Loopy

and Little Gee.

We're heroes,

we three.

In the park

in the dark

by the lake

and the bridge,

that's when we see

where we want to be,

me and Loopy

and Little Gee.

WHOOPEE!

And we swing

and we slide

and we dance

and we jump

and we chase

all over the place,

me and Loopy

and Little Gee,

the Big Three!

And then
the THING comes!
YAAAAA
AAAIII
OOOOOEEEEEEE!

RUN RUN RUN
shouts Little Gee
to Loopy and me
and we
flee,
me and Loopy
and Little Gee,
scared three.

Back where we've come
through the park
in the dark
and the THING
is roaring
and following,
see?
After me and Loopy
and Little Gee,
we three.

Up to the house,
to the stair,
to the bed
where we ought to be,
me and Loopy
and Little Gee,
safe as can be,
all three.